A WOODLAND MYSTERY™

The Forgotten Hiding Place

A WOODLAND MYSTERY
By Irene Schultz

The Wright Group®

To kindly neighbors who care about each
other

The Forgotten Hiding Place
©2000 Wright Group Publishing Inc.
Text by Irene Schultz
Cover illustration by Meg Aubrey
Cameo illustrations by Taylor Bruce
Interior illustrations by Cheryl Kirk Knoll and Adam Weiskind

Woodland Mysteries™
© Wright Group Publishing, Inc.

The Wright Group
19201 120th Avenue NE
Bothell, WA 98011
www.WrightGroup.com

Printed in the United States of America

10 9 8 7 6 5 4 3 2 1

ISBN: 0-322-01963-X
ISBN: 0-322-02376-9 (6-pack)

What family solves mysteries ... has adventures all over the world ... and loves oatmeal cookies?

It's the Woodlanders!

Sammy Westburg (10 years old)
His sister Kathy Westburg (13)
His brother Bill Westburg (14)
His best friend Dave Briggs (16)
His best grown-up friend Mrs. Tandy
And Mop, their little dog!

The children all lost their parents, but with Mrs. Tandy have made their own family.

Why are they called the Woodlanders? Because they live in a big house in the Bluff Lake woods. On Woodland Street!

Together they find fun, mystery, and adventure. What are they up to now?

Read on!

Meet the Woodlanders!

Sammy Westburg
Sammy is a ten-year-old wonder! He's big for his fifth-grade class, and big-mouthed, too. He has wild hair and makes awful spider faces. Even so, you can't help liking him.

Bill Westburg
Bill, fourteen, is friendly and strong, and only one inch taller than his brother Sammy. He loves Sammy, but pokes him to make him be quiet! He's in junior high.

Kathy Westburg
Kathy, thirteen, is small, shy, and smart. She wants to be a doctor some day! She loves to be with Dave, and her brothers kid her about it. She's in junior high, too.

Dave Briggs

Dave, sixteen, is tall and blond. He can't walk, so he uses a wheelchair and drives a special car. He likes coaching high-school sports, solving mysteries, and reading. And Kathy!

Mrs. Tandy

Sometimes the kids call her Mrs. T. She's Becky Tandy, their tall, thin, caring friend. She's always ready for a new adventure, and for making cookies!

Mop

Mop is the family's little tan dog. Sometimes they have to leave him behind with friends. But he'd much rather be running after Sammy.

Table of Contents

Chapter 1:
Mr. Moon's Lost Family

Sammy Westburg, ten, jumped up from the dining room table.

He started singing, "Done! Done! Done! The bozo bills are done!"

He hopped around in time to his song.

His brother Bill, fourteen, and his sister Kathy, thirteen, joined in.

Dave Briggs, sixteen, followed them in his wheelchair.

Then Mrs. Tandy stood up.

She danced and hopped with the others.

She held the bills, ready to mail, in the air.

Mop, their shaggy, tan dog, began barking and jumping.

Finally, Dave left the parade. He looked at his watch.

He said, "We've been writing checks and addressing envelopes for two hours.

"What a way to spend a beautiful October morning!

"Let's get outside and take a little walk."

Sammy said, "Why don't we pick out our favorite trees, like last year.

"And let's find acorns to throw into our woods."

Bill said, "Should we pick up shag bark hickory nuts?"

Sammy said, "Forget THAT.

"Remember how I picked up a whole potato sack full once, where we used to live?

"And the husks made black marks on the sack ... and our fingers and nails got dyed black taking the husks off? Ugh!

"The nuts were SO hard to crack ... and then we ended up giving them to the squirrels."

Mrs. Tandy said, "Look, kids, it's eleven o'clock.

"How about this for an idea? We put these bills out for the mail carrier to pick up.

"Then we make a lunch. We walk until we get hungry. We eat whenever we want to."

Usually quiet Kathy spoke up right away.

She said, "I love it!

"I'll make peanut butter and jelly sandwiches."

Dave said, "I'll help Kathy. Bill, why don't you and Sammy pack up some fruit. And something to drink. And napkins."

Mrs. Tandy said, "I'll get the picnic quilt ... and paper plates and cups ... and a basket."

Fifteen minutes later they were ready.

Dave said, "Put the quilt under me. I'll sit on it so we won't have to carry it."

He lifted himself up a little to make room.

Then he said, "Now you can put the basket on my lap."

Sammy raced outside to the front yard.

He shouted, "I'll beat you to the stop sign, Bill!"

Bill shouted back, "Huh! In your dreams, baby brother."

Bill shot straight through their woods to the corner.

He got to the stop sign far ahead of Sammy.

Then Bill turned to face him.

But Sammy didn't stop running.

He ran right at Bill.

At the last moment, Bill stepped aside and Sammy went skidding past him ... and into a pile of leaves.

Sammy stood up. He said, "I LET you win, Bill."

Then he smiled. "I feel a lot better now. I just HATE doing the bills.

"The only good part is, I get to put on the stamps.

"And I love stamps, even everyday stamps.

"Every time I go past the post office, I buy a stamp for my stamp collection. A commemorative."

He said the word like this: cuh- MEM-er-uh-tiv.

Bill said, "Your commemorative stamp collection is really good. I love the ones that have sports heroes.

"I'd like to start a commemorative collection, too."

They crossed the street kitty-corner.

They walked toward a little yellow house tucked into a small woods.

Mrs. Tandy said, "Mr. Moon's house always looks so sweet in there ... like a bird's nest."

Kathy said sadly, "I'm so sorry he died. He was so nice."

Mrs. Tandy said, "I wonder who owns his house now."

Sammy said, "I know who.

"He told me he was leaving it to his only granddaughter, April. He called her little April Moon.

"And she gets everything else he owned, too.

"He said she was very little and very sweet and darling."

Bill said, "If she's so sweet, where is she? How come she never came to Bluff Lake to visit him?"

Sammy said, "Because, smarty-pants, she couldn't.

"Mr. Moon's son, Jeff, got into trouble a long time ago.

"He was supposed to go fight in Vietnam.

"But he decided it wasn't right to go to war ... unless Congress declared war first.

"He said he loved his country, but the war wasn't legal.

"He figured he had to leave the U.S. ... or be put in jail.

"So one night he took his wife and little April and went away.

"Some people called him a coward. Some people said he was brave."

Bill said, "How terrible for Mr. Moon."

Sammy said, "All Mr. Moon had left was a letter from Jeff.

"It said Jeff and his family would always love him. There was no return address."

Kathy said, "You mean they left? And he never saw them again?"

Chapter 2:
The Truck Driver

Sammy said, "Well, Mr. Moon had an idea
where they MIGHT be.

"In Canada.

"But he knew his son wanted to stay hidden.

"So he never tried to get in touch with him."

Kathy said, "I bet it broke his heart.

"He lost a son, a daughter-in-law ... and his only grandchild."

Dave said, "But wait a minute! How could he leave his house and his things to her?

"He didn't even know she was still alive.

"Or where a lawyer could find her. Or what she's like, after thirty years."

Sammy said, "That's the greatest thing about it. He found out where she was!

"He got a letter from little April a month ago. It was just a week before he died.

"He and I were trading stamps at his

house when the letter came.

"He showed it to me. Then he went straight to his lawyer and wrote a will leaving everything to her.

"And he wrote to her that very night."

Mrs. Tandy said, "Well, that's wonderful! How come she wrote at last?"

Dave said, "I bet I can guess. I bet her mom and dad had both died.

"So she didn't have to be afraid anymore that her dad would go to jail. And she had no other family but her grandpa."

Sammy said, "You're exactly right. You should be a detective, Dave.

"You should have seen Mr. Moon when he got that letter.

"I think it was the happiest day in his life.

"The letter was addressed to 'Papa Mugsy Moon.'

13

"That's what she called him when she was little."

Kathy asked, "What did she say? It's a wonder she remembered him at all."

Sammy said, "She said her parents kept his picture near her bed. She said they talked about him every day.

"She said that her dad had become a medic.

"He worked in far-off parts of Canada, helping people get to a hospital.

"Now that he was dead, April wanted to come home to her grandpa.

"And she wanted to live in Bluff Lake again."

Bill said, "And now Mr. Moon's dead, too. Does she know?"

Sammy said, "I don't know.

"And I've told you everything I DO know. So it's time for more important things."

Then he slapped Bill on the arm.

He ran away shouting, "Gotcha!" and kept right on running.

Bill chased him to the end of the block.

Mop tried to run after them, but Kathy held his leash.

Partway down the next block, Sammy turned back toward Bill.

He stretched his eyes and mouth with both hands.

He made his terrible spider face.

He shouted, "Billy is a baby! Billy is an inch worm! Billy can't catch me-e-e!" and he ran some more.

But suddenly, he turned. He ran straight toward Bill.

He shouted, "Bill! Stop! Wait there!

"Look what's coming ... a moving van!"

He and Bill ran back to the rest of the family.

They watched as the huge truck thundered up the street ... and turned right into Mr. Moon's driveway!

The driver set the brake and climbed down.

Sammy elbowed Bill and said, "Let's go

see if he knows when little April's getting here."

The driver was medium tall. He was built a little like a football player ... with wide shoulders and thick legs.

He wore jeans, a leather jacket, and a baseball cap.

He walked right into Mr. Moon's woods.

He turned left up the path to the door. Then ...

HE TOOK OUT A KEY, OPENED THE DOOR, STEPPED INSIDE, AND CLOSED IT!

Bill said, "Wait a minute! I never saw a mover do that ... go inside without the owner."

Mrs. Tandy said, "He wouldn't even know where to unload."

Dave said, "I can't imagine he was supposed to go in."

Kathy said, "Maybe we should report this to Chief Hemster."

Sammy said, "Report? NO WAY! I'm going after him!"

Before they could stop him, Sammy ran up to the door.

He banged on it. No answer.

The Woodlanders caught up to him.

He banged again.

This time they heard footsteps inside.

The truck driver opened the door.

Sammy shot off his mouth the minute he saw the driver.

"What are you doing in there?" he shouted.

"What right do you have to go inside?

"You're in BIG trouble, buddy!"

Chapter 3:
I'm Calling the Police

Mrs. Tandy put her hand on Sammy's shoulder. She tried to calm him.

She said to the trucker, "We were worried when we saw you go inside.

"You see, the house belonged to our friend, Morrison Moon.

"We aren't sure you should be inside until Mr. Moon's granddaughter arrives."

But Sammy wasn't any calmer. He stuck out his chin.

Then he pointed his finger at the truck driver.

He said, "I'm calling the police!

"Chief Hemster will keep an eye on you until little April gets here!"

Then Bill noticed that the trucker's cheeks had two thin lines running down them ... lines that looked like dried tears.

Bill said, "Hey ... who are you, anyway?"

Instead of answering, the driver raised a thick, muscled arm ... and lifted the baseball cap a little way off his head.

A mound of black, silky hair spilled down.

It was tied on top with a flattened pink bow.

THE TRUCK DRIVER WAS A WOMAN!

She grinned and said, "I bet you're the Woodlanders.

"My grandpa wrote me about you. He said Sammy was his special friend.

"You. Big talker. You must be Sammy."

She wrapped a strong arm around Sammy and hugged him.

Sammy thought, "This is what it's like when a bear gets you!"

The truck driver said, "It's me, little April Moon.

"But I'm big April Moon now.

"And this must be Bill. Shake." She gave Bill her hand.

Bill shook it and thought, "Why, it's almost as big as a catcher's mitt!"

Sammy exclaimed, "You mean YOU'RE his little April?"

"Wow! Your grandpa sure would be surprised to see you now!"

April Moon's mouth drooped. Tears rose in her eyes.

She said, "I guess it's lucky Papa Mugsy didn't see me before he passed away."

She sniffed and wiped her eyes with a huge red hanky.

22

"I bet the sight of me would have made him pretty sad. I've changed so much."

Sammy said, "Wait, that's not what I meant. I said he'd be surprised; I didn't say sad!

"I meant he'd be surprised that you grew up strong and smart enough to drive a TRUCK! He'd be GLAD! Please don't cry!"

Sammy patted her hand. He felt so terrible that for once in his life he stopped talking.

Mrs. Tandy stepped forward. She put her arms around April.

She said, "Why, he'd have been so proud of you."

Bill said, "We hope you'll be our neighbor for a long time. Forever, even."

April Moon began to smile just a little.

She said, "I hope so, too ... but I'm mixed up about it.

"First, I got the sweetest letter from my grandpa. I was surprised and thrilled!

"Then his lawyer called, four days later. A man named Sol Fine.

"I was packing everything I owned, ready to come live with Mugsy at last. But Mr. Fine told me Grandpa had died.

"I cried for a week.

"I didn't have enough money to fly here for his funeral.

"I barely had enough for gas to drive the truck here.

"With Mugsy gone, I almost thought I should stay in Canada.

"Then I decided to come, at least to see my first home again.

"You see, a few years back my dad bought this truck. He and I both drove it.

"But when Dad got sick, I stayed home to take care of him. That used up most of our savings.

"After he died, it was just me and the truck. I made my living with it. I drove it all over Canada."

She sighed. "I've made some long drives, but this was the worst. It's so far from my part of Canada.

"I was afraid a woman alone might have trouble. So I hid my long hair in this baseball cap. That way, I looked like a man.

"I locked the van and stayed in it at night.

"I was scared so I didn't sleep very well. So I'm pretty tired.

"And I'm dirty as a pig.

"But I made it."

Bill felt sorry for her.

He said, "I bet you could use a bath.

And some lunch.

"We packed a HUGE lunch, right there in that basket.

"Why not come across the street to our house and get cleaned up?

"And then we can all eat in our backyard, on Leaf Hill."

April Moon said, "A hill? In your backyard?

Mrs. Tandy said, "It's really only about twenty years of piled-up leaves.

"But it's a lot of fun to picnic on it."

Dave said, "We can help you move into your home later."

Kathy said, "I bet you could use a little nap, too."

Sammy said, "We want to make sure you're OK after your trip.

"So it's all decided, right?"

April Moon looked at each of their friendly faces.

Then suddenly, she covered her own
face with her huge hands.

She sat down right there on her
driveway and bawled like a baby.

Chapter 4:
You Look Like a Million Dollars!

April just sat there crying.

Mop was the first to think of something to do.

He stretched out on his leash and licked April's face.

Then Dave wheeled up right next to her.

He looked at her and put his hand softly on her shoulder.

Next, Bill sat down on the driveway on her other side.

The rest of the Woodlanders sat with her, too.

Finally, all six people, and Mop, were sitting in a circle.

No one was able to think of the right thing to say.

Finally, Sammy patted his stomach.

He said, "I'm getting hungry."

Then he said, "Maybe we should eat right here."

April lifted her head.

She said, "Look at us. All sitting in a circle on the driveway." She giggled.

The others began to giggle.

April said, "I'm so sorry I'm being such a big baby."

Mrs. Tandy said, "Why, you're all worn out, honey.

"Worn out from sadness ... and worrying about money ... and sleeping in your truck.

"You need time to put yourself back together.

"Come along. Get into some clean clothes and have lunch.

April frowned and said, "I wouldn't be good company.

"And I'd make your lunch late while you waited for me.

"And I bet you were looking forward to a good walk, too.

"I should be tough enough to take care of myself.

"And I have no way to repay you for

31

your kindness.

"And the worst thing is, I'm not even related to you.

"You'd be going to a lot of trouble for a stranger. You don't even know me."

Bill said, "Don't say that. We DO know you.

"Well, anyway, we know how you feel ... just the way we felt before we got together.

"You've lost your family, just like we did."

Kathy added, "We had to make a new family after we came here. That's how come we all live together in one house."

Sammy said, "Maybe, until you're settled, WE could be your family ... if you want us."

April said, "I sure do!"

She went to her moving van. She opened the back door.

She climbed inside to get two suitcases. Sammy poked Bill.

He whispered, "Can you see inside the truck?

"It's as big as a house in there, but it's mostly empty.

"Just a little table and some chairs and some boxes.

"Gee, she hardly owns anything except the truck."

Bill whispered, "It's a lucky thing Mr. Moon had furniture."

Dave said, "April, lay your bags over the arms of my chair. I'll carry them."

Bill took the picnic basket.

They led her kitty-corner, across the street to their house.

They showed her where to take a bath and change her clothes.

Kathy poured bubble bath powder into the tub. She ran the water.

Fluffy bubbles puffed up on top of the water. She announced, "Your bath is ready whenever you are!"

Then she and the rest of the family went into the dining room at the other end of the house.

■   ■   ■

A half-hour later, the door from the hall opened.

There stood a fresh, clean, lovely-looking woman.

She wore a flowered blouse and a full skirt.

She carried a bunch of dirty clothes in one hand.

Sammy shouted, "WOW! April, is that you?

"You look like a million dollars!"

April grinned. She said, "I'm sorry I took so long. I was pretty dirty!

"First, I soaked in that sweet bubble bath.

"But after a while, I took a look at the bath water. It was disGUSTing!

"The bubbles were gone! The water looked like gray soup.

"So I opened the drain and let the water run out. Then I washed the tub.

"Then I turned on the shower and washed myself all over again.

"Finally, when I knew I was REALLY clean, I dried myself off and got dressed.

"I feel like a new person!"

Mrs. Tandy walked into the hall.

She opened a small door near the floor.

She said, "Here, April, drop your dirty clothes in here.

"They'll slide straight down into the laundry room."

Bill said, "I'll put them into the washing machine."

April said, "Thanks so much. It'll feel like you're washing away some of my troubles ... along with a week's worth of dirt."

But at that very moment, the front doorbell rang.

How were they to know it was a brand new trouble coming to call?

Chapter 5:
Mean Mouth

Sammy shouted, "I'LL GET IT!"

He raced past Bill to open the door.

There stood a woman in a beautiful gray suit.

She was about as tall as April.

She wore a spotless white blouse and pearl earrings.

Her long, smooth, blonde hair was perfectly cut to show off her tanned face.

Her makeup was so good she could have been a model.

But Sammy thought she looked like a killer bee!

She looked MAD!

Mop took one look and ran off to hide under Sammy's bed.

Sammy backed up toward Bill and whispered, "It's that lady from across the street ... Mean Mouth."

The woman caught sight of Mrs. Tandy and said, "Thank goodness there's an adult here.

"I'm Janet Adams. You must have heard my name."

She spoke very clearly.

38

"I live in the beautiful, gray stone English house. Next to old Mr. Moon's.

Mrs. Tandy said, "Yes, I know. Can we help you?"

Mrs. Adams said, "I have a problem.

"You must have noticed that I keep up my home perfectly.

"It makes the whole neighborhood look nice.

"Well, someone has left a huge, ugly moving van parked at Mr. Moon's place.

"It's muddy and awful looking! Just awful!

"And the worst thing of all is the van is parked right next door to me!

"Now, there was one good thing about Mr. Moon.

"He didn't have a truck. Anyway, his house is hidden back in the woods.

"But not with this truck in the driveway! Anyone can see it!

"It must be towed ... fast. I'm giving a party tomorrow."

April stepped forward.

Mrs. Tandy thought, "She reminds me of a big, friendly dog walking up to a yapping poodle."

April said, "Sorry I caused you trouble. The truck is mine.

"And I'm sorry it's so dirty.

"I was five long days on the road. It was bound to pick up an awful lot of muck.

"But it'll be gone tomorrow.

"I'm going to park it out near the highway.

"I'm going to be your new neighbor. My name is April Moon. Morrison Moon was my grandfather. He left his house to me."

Janet Adams looked shocked. She stood perfectly still.

Then she forced her mouth into a
fake smile. But her eyes weren't really
smiling.

She said, "YOU'RE April Moon? Mr.
Moon's granddaughter? You're a ...
TRUCK DRIVER?

"And you're going to LIVE in Bluff Lake?   Next door?

"Well ... that is ... not that there's anything WRONG with truck drivers.

"In fact ... I suppose they might really be quite nice ... although I've never met one myself.

"And perhaps we can find you more ladylike work, once you have moved in next door."

April said, "That's very kind of you, Mrs. Adams, but I really love my work.

"I have a chance to travel.   I help a lot of people.

"I love to drive.   And the pay is good, if you work hard.

"I figure it's ladylike enough for me.

"I'm proud to be doing it."

Janet Adams pressed her lips together and smiled an even BIGGER fake smile.

She said, "Well, my dear, don't give

your truck another thought. Since it's yours, it's perfectly all right exactly where it is.

"So Mr. Moon's place is yours now?

"You'll be un-loading today and tomorrow, I guess.

"I'll be over at eight in the morning to help un-pack.

"And I'll bring along coffee and rolls."

April said, "Thanks. That's nice of you.

"But there's nothing much I have to un-pack.

"I'd love your company tomorrow morning, though."

Janet Adams said, "Oh, I'll give you more than my company. I'm going to help you decorate.

"I ... uh ... I promised your dear grandfather I'd decorate for him. So, now, of course, I'm going to help you ... for free.

Woodland Street

Sunset Road

 Woodlanders' House

 Moons' House

 Janet Adams' House

 Woods

N

W E

S

44

"After all, what are good friends for?"

Then she leaned past April and said, "You Woodlanders don't need to come by tomorrow."

She waved a perfect hand with long, blood-red nails, and left.

April said, "That sure is one take-over lady! But please don't let her scare you away."

Sammy said, "She won't scare ME away. When I grow up, I think I might be a truck driver like you. I LOVE your truck!"

April said, "Well, Mrs. Adams sure didn't love it.

"But she cooled down, and she acted extra-friendly when I said it was mine.

"Even so, I feel she doesn't like me. Just a gut feeling."

Mrs. Tandy said, "That's one smart gut.

"That lady doesn't like ANYONE ...

except herself.

"I never saw her do anything unless she wanted something in return. But of course, maybe this time is different."

Sammy whispered to Bill, "Don't you believe it!"

Chapter 6:
April's Life

Bill said, "Let's forget about Mrs. Adams."

Sammy said, "Good idea!   Let's just eat!"

He grabbed the basket and raced out to the little leaf hill.

Mop came out from under the bed and ran out with them.

Mrs. Tandy handed fruit and drinks all around.

Kathy gave out one and a half sandwiches to each person.

She said, "I had ten sandwiches made from before. So there's one sandwich left over."

Sammy pulled out his pocket knife and cut that sandwich into six parts.

When they were finished eating, Sammy said, "I have to sharpen my knife some time.

"It got dull when I scraped mud off my shoes yesterday."

Bill said, "Sammy! Did you clean it when you were done?"

Sammy put an angel smile on his face.

He said, "Don't worry, I wiped it clean ... on a big juicy worm like this one!"

He dropped a worm onto Bill's bare arm.

Quick as a wink, Bill dropped it back into Sammy's lap.

Dave said, "No worm wars, guys. It's time to hear about April's life after she left our town ... when she was four."

Bill said, "What do you remember about your life back then, April?"

April said, "I remember playing with Papa Mugsy.

"I had to call him 'Mugsy' because I couldn't say 'Morrison.'

"I remember he used to show me his stamp collection.

"And we used to play hide-and-go-seek.

"And I remember being on a plane with my folks.

"And I remember the train ride across Canada."

Bill asked, "Where did you settle?"

April said, "We settled in north western Canada. My dad got work there, cleaning up in a hospital at night.

"And he went to medic classes in the daytime.

"In a few years, he was driving an ambulance.

"Finally, he had studied enough to become a full-time medic.

"He'd drive anywhere, day or night. He'd go out in any kind of weather to help people.

"And my mom became a housekeeper in a huge house.

"We all got to live there because of her work."

Kathy said, "They sound like wonderful people."

April said, "They were. But then, in my third year in college, Mom got very sick.

"I decided to leave school. I helped Dad care for her until she passed away.

"We were left with a ton of bills to pay.

"I decided to stick with Dad instead of going back to college.

51

"He wanted to get away from sickness and hospitals.

"So we got together every cent we could.

"We made a down payment on the moving truck.

"We both took a good course in truck driving.

"Then we took to the road.

"We drove all over western Canada, moving furniture."

Mrs. Tandy said, "You're a strong, fine woman, April."

April answered, "I don't feel so strong right now.

"I could lie down on this quilt and sleep like a baby."

Dave said, "Great idea. Do it.

"We can take in the lunch stuff. After you wake up, we can help you empty the truck."

Some time later, April woke and looked at her watch.

The Woodlanders saw her from the kitchen window. They rushed out the back door.

Mrs. Tandy said, "Your work clothes are all clean and dry."

April changed, and they went to her truck. They helped her carry everything into Mr. Moon's house.

April said, "I'd like to get my things into drawers.

"But Mugsy's things are still in them ... and I don't want to clear them out in a hurry.

"I'd like to go through them carefully. I'll know him better when I know how he lived."

Kathy said, "Why don't we put your things into the drawers, and his into boxes?

53

"We can carry the boxes out to the garage.

"Then you can look through them sometime during the week."

April said, "Thanks, that's a wonderful idea!"

Later, they made up her bed. By then, it was getting dark.

Sammy said, "Hey, why don't you sleep at our place tonight!

"We have a monster of a jigsaw puzzle. You can help put it together. You'll be doing us a favor."

The others loved the idea, and so did April.

So she grabbed some clothes and locked up.

They all went back to the Woodlanders' house.

Much later that night, in the dark ... someone tiptoed into April's garage.

54

Chapter 7:
The Take-Over Lady

The next morning, Sammy woke up to the sound of rain.

He jumped out of bed in his bright red pajamas.

He began singing at the top of his lungs, "RAIN, RAIN, GO AWAY!"

He ran through the hall. Mop ran with him, barking.

Sammy thought, "I bet THAT got Mrs. Tandy and Kathy and April up!"

Then he ran down to Bill and Dave's room.

He started shouting over again, "RAIN, RAIN, GO AWAY! COME AGAIN SOME OTHER DAY!"

Bill had heard Sammy the first time. He was ready.

Sammy threw the door open.

SPLAT! A wet washcloth landed on his face!

Bill jumped down from his bed and ran to the bathroom.

He locked the door before Sammy got there.

Sammy banged on it and shouted,

"Open up! I won't do anything!"

Bill shouted, "Yeah, like I believe THAT!

"Go take Mop out before he has an accident."

Dave gave a little laugh from his bed.

Sammy threw the wet washcloth onto Dave's head.

Sammy shouted, "There, now I'm even with you guys!" He ran off.

Laughing, Dave lifted himself into his wheelchair.

Five minutes later, they were all dressed. They drank orange juice and ate waffles.

Then they all hurried over to April's house.

Dave took his hand-controlled van.

He followed April to her truck's new parking place. Then she rode with him back to her house.

Sammy was standing out in the rain when they returned.

He shouted, "What took you so long? Come into the garage! Wait till you see!"

"When you left, I looked in to make sure everything was dry.

"Look!"

He pointed to the boxes of Mr. Moon's things.

April said, "I know we left them in a neat row ... with the flaps tucked in.

"Now they're every which way, with the flaps pulled out."

Sammy said, "And someone searched through them. They're all messed up inside.

"Mrs. Tandy's in the house with Kathy and Bill.

"They're checking to see if any of your things look messed up."

The rest of the Woodlanders came out to the garage.

Bill said, "Someone's been in the house, too."

Mrs. Tandy said, "Do you remember how carefully we made the bed? Like a bed in a furniture store?

"We wanted it to be so nice for you, April.

"Well, you can tell that someone was

sitting on it. They smoothed it over, but the blankets sag a little."

Just then, they heard high heels tapping past the garage.

April called, "Mrs. Adams, is that you out there?

"Come into the garage."

Janet Adams called back, "I'll just go right on into the house, April dear."

Sammy said, "'DEAR'! How come she calls you 'dear'?

"All she ever calls me is 'LITTLE BOY'!"

Bill said, "Don't let it get to you, Sammy. She calls me 'little boy,' too."

They went into the house. But they didn't see Mrs. Adams.

Then they heard the tapping of high heels above them.

They walked to the stairway.

Mrs. Adams came to the top of the steps. She said, "I came up here to decide what needs to be done first."

She was carrying a white bag and a jar of instant coffee.

She said, "I brought four sweet rolls with me.

"That's two for April and two for me.

"April and I need time alone to talk about decorating.

"I'm sure the rest of you won't be staying."

All of a sudden, the family felt like outsiders.

Bill said, "Good-bye then, April. Call us when you're free."

Dave said, "We can drive you around when you need us.

"You'll want to get a phone. And go to city hall to get your voter's card.

"And you'll need to do some grocery shopping."

But April said, "Just a minute! I want

61

you ALL to stay.

"Mrs. Adams, we've already had breakfast. So four rolls are plenty.

"Just cut them in half, and make eight pieces."

Mrs. Adams frowned.

She said, "Oh, all right, I suppose. I'll make us some coffee.

"You boys, and you, little girl, keep out of the way."

She walked into the kitchen. She got a plate for the rolls and some cups. She opened a drawer and got spoons.

She opened another cupboard and took down a box of sweetener.

Suddenly, Dave said, "Hey, Mrs. Adams, you seem to know where everything is.

"You've been in this house before, haven't you? A lot."

Sammy said, "I'm surprised. I didn't know you knew Mr. Moon at all."

Chapter 8:
Hello, Mr. Fine

Janet Adams said, "Why, I knew Mr. Moon very well."

"He gave me a house key, we were such good friends."

Mrs. Tandy said, "Then maybe that explains what we found here. It must have been you who came into the house last night."

Janet Adams's eyes opened wide with surprise.

She gasped, "I? ... No! ... How? ... "

She realized they were all staring at her.

Her eyes darted left and right. She looked like an animal backed into a corner. There was no way out.

She breathed deeply and said, "I ... know ... how ... very hard it is to make yourself at home in any new place, April.

"So I DID stop in ... to make sure your lights were working ... and the furnace was on ... and the water was clear."

April smiled. She said, "That was mighty kind of you. But the Woodlanders

64

had everything set up fine."

Sammy said, "Well, why did you go into the garage?"

Mrs. Adams said, "I wanted to make sure that everything was safe from mice out there. So I stirred through the boxes.

"And now, April, you can begin the REAL work of making this into a lovely home ... just as your grandfather wished.

"I'll sort out every cupboard.

"I'll find new ways to place all the furniture.

"I'll put the bookshelves into good order.

"I'll clean out the attic.

"I'll make the basement neat.

"I'll find a place for everything in the garage.

"I'll choose colors for the walls, and cloth for curtains.

"I won't overlook one little corner of this house."

At that moment, there was a knock on the door.

April opened it.

There stood a tall, well-dressed man, about forty years old.

He smiled and said, "Hello. April? Glad to meet you.

"I'm Sol Fine, your grandfather's lawyer.

"Welcome to Bluff Lake. I want to welcome you and visit for a bit ... if you have time?

"And set a date for you to read your grandpa's will."

He noticed Mrs. Tandy and the family.

He said, "Hiya, Becky. How are you doing? And how are the rest of you Woodlanders?"

Then he said, "And who's your other visitor, April?"

April said, "I'm surprised you haven't met each other. This is Janet Adams. She was a close friend of Papa Mugsy's."

Mrs. Adams said, "Hello. But I'm sorry, I'm sure you won't want to visit now.

"April and I are just going to work on her house.

"Maybe you could come back another time."

But April said, "Oh, no, don't go. Stay for coffee.

"We were just going to have sweet rolls, too. In fact, we have exactly eight pieces.

"I love to talk to anyone who knew Mugsy."

Mr. Fine laughed. "You called him 'Mugsy'? I bet he loved that. No wonder he was so glad to hear from you at last.

"He'd be so happy that you're getting settled in here."

They all moved into the dining room. April said, "But maybe I CAN'T settle here for good.

"I might not be able to earn enough money to live in Bluff Lake."

Mr. Fine said, "Don't worry. That's all taken care of.

"Your grandfather left you some money.

"And of course, you can sell his stamps. I believe they're worth a small fortune."

April said, "His stamps? I had no idea he still had them."

She poured coffee and asked, "Would any of you kids like some?"

Now, Sammy HATED coffee. But he said, "I'd LOVE some!" He shot Mrs. Adams a look that meant, "I'm no little boy!"

But Bill said, "Sammy! You are NOT going to have coffee! I brought juice for us kids."

They pulled chairs up to the dining room table.

April said, "The stamp collection is such good news.

"You know, though, I wouldn't sell ALL of it. I'd sell only the most valuable stamps, but I'd keep all the rest. I love them.

"I remember what fun Papa Mugsy and I had looking at them. To this day I carry a magnifying glass he gave me."

She got her purse to show it to them. It was a little magnifying glass, only as big as a quarter. It was in a worn leather case.

She said, "I remember we soaked the corners of envelopes in water to get the stamps off.

"We worked on them right there at the kitchen sink.

"Then we dried all the stamps on newspaper, face down.

"In fact, I collect stamps to this day. My grandpa showed me how beautiful they are.

"Where are his stamps? I'm dying to see them again."

The lawyer said, "Your grandfather didn't tell me where they were.

"He just said to tell you they're in the same old place."

April said, "I don't have ANY memory of where he used to keep the stamps! Not a clue!"

Chapter 9:
Good-bye, Mr. Fine

April groaned, "I feel so stupid, but I don't remember."

Bill said, "You're not stupid. You were only four years old when you left.

"It's too bad your grandpa didn't leave a note."

Mrs. Adams said, "Well, he didn't, so that's that."

Dave said, "Sammy, you must have seen Mr. Moon's stamps a million times. Didn't he ever say where he kept them?"

Sammy said, "No, he always had them on the table when I came. Or I'd wait in the front room while he left to get them."

Janet Adams said, "Well, it just so happens you're all wasting your time with this talk.

"Mr. Moon told me he sold them, some time ago."

She said, "He just didn't remember that when he spoke to you. After all, he was very old."

Sammy blurted out, "Old doesn't mean STUPID, Mrs. Adams!

74

"If he said those stamps are here somewhere, they ARE."

Janet Adams said, "You need to learn manners, little boy!

"You think you know better than adults."

Mr. Fine said, "Oh, but Sammy IS probably right about the stamps, Mrs. Adams.

"Mr. Moon's mind seemed sound when we talked."

Janet Adams got up. She smiled at Mr. Fine. She batted her long eyelashes at him.

She even reached over and patted his hand.

She said, "Well, well! I can't sit around here all day. I'll run along now. But I do hope we meet again, Mr. Fine. It was lovely meeting you.

"I'll come back tomorrow, April, when

we can be alone. Then we can really start working on plans for the house."

Sammy growled, "It feels nice to me just the way it is."

Janet Adams walked out with her nose in the air.

April said to the others, "I feel bad that she's not polite to you young people. Does she have children of her own?"

Mrs. Tandy said, "Oh, yes. Two girls. She likes to say a woman's place is with her family.

"But she sends her children to school out of town.

"She's a widow. I heard that her father pays for the school.

"She sees her kids during vacations only."

April said, "Well, do you think she might be right about the stamps? She sounded awfully sure of it."

Sammy said, "Oh yeah? She's sure they're sold?

"Then how come your grandpa and I looked at them together the day before he died?"

April gasped, "Do you really mean that?"

Sammy said, "Sure! Right here at this table.

"We were measuring perforations."

He said the word like this: per-fer-AY-shunz.

"You know, those tiny holes between stamps. Where you fold them and tear them apart.

"Well, different stamps have different perforations. We used his perforation gauge."

He said the word like this: GAJE.

Sammy said, "The gauge tells how far apart the holes are.

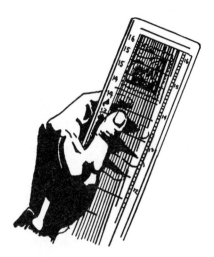

"So Janet Adams is lying ... and besides, she's rude as a skunk!"

Mr. Fine laughed and said, "Well, she's pretty. Maybe she thinks she doesn't have to be honest or polite."

April said, "Well, I suppose I'm lucky she's nice to me. I'd feel bad if a close friend of Mugsy's didn't like me."

Dave said, "Are you sure you want her over here when you're away?"

April said, "In my business, I'll be gone

a lot. She could keep an eye on things for me.

"And I'd be so glad if you Woodlanders would check on things when you can."

She slipped a key off her key ring. She handed it to Dave.

Mr. Fine got up to leave. He looked across the room.

He said, "I agree with Sammy, April. This house looks awfully nice to me the way it is.

"I want to sit in that rocking chair, myself."

April said, "Well, the house looks like heaven to me. But then, what do I know? I'm only a truck driver, not a decorator."

While she was talking, she took a good look at Mr. Fine.

She smiled. She liked his hair. And the kind, smart look on his face.

Mr. Fine picked up his briefcase and said, "Well, I'll be on my way.

"I'm going to call on Mrs. Adams. Maybe I can stir up her memory about where Mr. Moon kept those stamps.

"Maybe she has a clue and doesn't realize it.

"I'll be back to see you soon, April. Then we can set a date to read the will."

April said, "Good-bye, Mr. Fine." She shut the door.

She said sadly, "Good-bye is exactly right.

"We won't be seeing Mr. Fine here again any time soon.

"He's got someone mighty pretty to spend his time with."

Sammy asked, "Well, then, with Mr. Fine and Mrs. Adams gone, what should WE do with the rest of the day?"

Chapter 10:
Spying on a Spy

April said, "Well, I'd better start getting all set up.

"I need to buy groceries ... and go to the post office ... and get a phone. And I have to sign up for voting.

"Can I take you up on your kind offer to drive me, Dave?"

Dave said, "Sure. And we can help carry groceries."

Mrs. Tandy said, "You'll have to count me out for a while.

"I'm meeting Chief Hemster. He and I are giving blood at ten o'clock. There's a special drive at the blood bank."

Sammy grinned and said, "Then I'd better go with you ... in case you feel faint when you see your boyfriend."

Mrs. Tandy laughed. "I've gone to the blood bank with Chief Hemster for years and years. I've never felt faint one single time!

"You're just thinking of the cookies they serve, Sammy. Would that have anything to do with your offer to come?"

Dave said, "I'll drop you and Sammy off."

Kathy, Bill, and April headed for Dave's car.

Bill and Sammy loaded the wheelchair in the back.

Then Bill happened to look up through the branches of a tree.

He saw Mrs. Adams standing on her balcony. She was holding something up to her eyes.

He poked Sammy and whispered, "Don't turn your head ... but take a look up at Mrs. Adams's balcony. What's she doing?"

Sammy whispered back, "I guess Mr. Fine didn't stay there long. She's alone. She's watching us with a pair of FIELD glasses!"

Kathy said, "I sure hope Mr. Fine's too smart to fall for her. Did you see how April looked at him? It was love at first sight!"

Bill whispered, "Well, Mrs. Adams is up to something.

"And her going into April's house last night? That seemed plenty fishy to me.

"I'm not going shopping. I'm sticking around here to keep an eye on her."

He turned to Dave and said, "I just thought of something I want to do. Can you and Kathy take April shopping without me?"

Then Sammy said, "I just thought of something, too. I guess I'll skip the blood bank."

So the others went off in the car.

Sammy and Bill hurried back to their house.

Bill grabbed two pairs of field glasses from the living room cupboard.

The boys went out their back door. They sneaked through the woods to the front.

They hid behind some trees and looked through the field glasses at Mrs. Adams's balcony.

Sammy said, "She's gone!"

Then they saw Mrs. Adams moving through April's woods.

They saw her sneak up to April's front door.

She un-locked it and disappeared inside.

Sammy said, "You'd think she'd be afraid of getting caught."

Bill said, "I guess she's pretty safe. All she'd have to say is she wanted more time to think about the decorating.

"I'm dying to see what she's doing in there. I have a feeling it doesn't have anything to do with decorating."

Sammy said, "Come on. Let's peek in the windows."

Before Bill could say anything, Sammy was across the street ... darting through April's woods like a squirrel.

Bill ran after him. He grabbed a sleeve of Sammy's jacket. Bill whispered, "She might see you!"

But Sammy shook free. He ran even closer to April's house. So Bill followed him.

The boys crawled along the side of April's house. They peeked into every window.

No sign of Mrs. Adams.

Bill said, "She's nowhere on the first floor. She must be upstairs again."

They went to the side of the house where they had started. They peeked in at the window that faced the stairway.

Sammy said, "Why would she be upstairs?"

Bill said, "You know, Sammy, it almost seems like she's looking for something."

Just then, they saw Mrs. Adams's feet at the top of the stairs.

They jumped away from the window.

They stood flat against the wall.

They held their breath, hoping she wouldn't see them.

A minute later, they heard noises from the downstairs bedroom.

Bill said, "What in the world is all that banging?"

Sammy said, "That's easy. It's dresser drawers being slammed shut.

"When you check to see if I've been snooping in your dresser, you open a drawer to look ... then SLAM!"

Bill said, "So, she IS searching for something! She sure doesn't have to look through drawers to decorate a house."

Just then, the drawer-slamming stopped.

Bill whispered, "Quick, hit the ground! She might be coming out!"

They threw themselves down into the thick leaves.

What if Mrs. Adams walked out the front door, right near them?

But they heard the back door slam.

Mrs. Adams's footsteps crunched through the leaves, back to her own house.

Bill whispered, "Come on, Sammy. We've got to talk to everyone else in the family. Fast."

Chapter 11:
She's Trying to Steal!

Sammy and Bill waited at the front of April's house.

Finally, Dave drove up. April and Kathy were in the backseat.

Sammy ran up to the van and called, "Do we have something to tell you! Wait till you hear THIS!"

Bill poked him in the ribs. He hissed, "Hush, Sammy!"

Sammy whispered, "Stop POKING me! What IS it?"

Bill whispered back, "Don't say anything in front of April.

"What if we aren't right? We don't have proof."

Sammy whispered, "OK. But I owe you a poke. A hard one."

Just then Chief Hemster and Mrs. Tandy arrived.

Mrs. Tandy handed a plastic bag to Sammy.

She said, "The woman at the blood bank sent these home for you."

Sammy said, "Chocolate chip! I can't wait till I get to give blood!"

Bill whispered a few words to Chief Hemster.

The chief said, "Well, Woodlanders, I need to talk to you.

"Let's go over to your house for a while."

April said, "But come back here for lunch.

"I'm throwing a little party to thank you for your help."

Back at their house, the boys told everyone what they had seen.

Bill said, "We don't have any proof ... but I'm sure Mrs. Adams is up to something!"

Kathy said, "Why don't we write down what we really know about her?"

Mrs. Tandy said, "Well, she's a widow with two girls, but she doesn't want them around."

Chief Hemster said, "Everyone knows

she's always complaining about her neighbors ... to the police and to everyone else.

"She even wrote to the town paper to complain about a neighbor. I thought she was talking about Mr. Moon."

Kathy said, "I remember that letter now! It was printed about a week before he died.

"She said that a neighbor's yard was all wild woods.

"She said that he should cut down the trees and put in a neat lawn like hers.

"She ended by calling him a stubborn old man."

Sammy said, "So how come she says they were such good friends?"

He hit the table and said, "Here's something else.

"Mr. Moon never said ANYTHING about her decorating his house.

"He never talked about her at all, except to laugh at that letter. He said she sounded like a spoiled brat!

"So I don't believe he EVER gave her a key.

"I'd like to know how she REALLY got it."

Dave said, "Add this to the list: Mrs. Adams is never nice to anyone ... but she's being extra friendly to April. I wonder why."

95

Bill said, "How about this: She spends a FORTUNE on clothes.

"I saw her at the store when we were shopping for Mrs. T's birthday. She bought a zillion dollars worth of clothes."

Sammy said, "Keeping up her house must cost a zillion.

"And parties and fancy cars cost another zillion.

"Where does she get all those zillions?"

Dave said, "She says she earns money decorating.

"Would that be enough to pay for what she spends?"

Mrs. Tandy said, "I hardly think it would be."

Just then, they heard a knock on the door.

Sammy ran to answer it.

There stood Mr. Fine. He said, "I stopped in at April's.

"She invited me to come to lunch. She said to tell you lunch is ready when you are."

Sammy pulled him inside. "You came at just the right time!

"You can help us get the lowdown on Janet Adams ...

"because we think she was snooping around at April's,

"and you should tell us what you know about her,

"unless you like her because she's pretty,

"... and you're too dumb to see how great April is!"

Bill said, "If Sammy's English teacher ever heard that sentence, she'd faint."

Sammy said, "You're jealous because you didn't say it."

Mr. Fine said, "Well, I HAVE heard some gossip about Mrs. Adams ... "

Mrs. Tandy said, "I heard that she seldom pays her bills. Once she let them pile up for almost two years.

"Then her dad felt so ashamed for her, HE paid the bills."

Kathy said, "Then she must be very short on money."

Bill said, "And she's a sneak and she tells lies."

Dave said, "And she's sneaking around looking for something in April's house."

Sammy said, "And I bet we all know what it is."

Chapter 12:
Mrs. Adams Is out
the Door

They all yelled together:

"MR. MOON'S STAMP COLLECTION!"

Sammy cried, "It must still be in the house!"

They rushed outside and over to April's.

Sammy ran in yelling, "Boy, do we have stuff to tell YOU!

"Mrs. Adams ... "

But he didn't get any further.

April said, "Sammy, do sit down and eat lunch.

"This is my first party in my new home."

Sammy banged down into a chair. He took a huge bite of a bacon and tomato sandwich.

Then he began talking again.

He said, "April, you've got to listen to us.

"You can't trust Mrs. Adams!

"You have to stop her from coming to your house."

They told her all about Mrs. Adams's spying and the letter to the paper.

April said, "It's plain she's up to no good.

"But I don't have proof. What can I say to her?"

Dave said, "Well, I know how we can get proof."

He told them his plan.

A minute later, Sammy dashed over to Mrs. Adams's house.

He pounded on her door.

She opened it and said, "What do YOU want?"

Sammy said, "April and we five Woodlanders are going walking. I thought you might want to go."

Mrs. Adams said, "With you children? Don't be stupid."

She slammed the door.

Sammy ran back to get the others for the walk.

Five minutes later, following Dave's

plan, they sneaked back inside ... with Mr. Fine and Chief Hemster following them.

They heard noises upstairs. Mrs. Adams was up there!

Silently, Dave wheeled into the big front-hall closet.

Mr. Fine and the chief hid behind the couch.

Kathy, April, and Mrs. Tandy sneaked into the downstairs bedroom.

Bill ducked behind an armchair.

But Sammy didn't hide. Dave had told him what to do.

First, he slammed the front door ... as if he had just come in.

Quickly, he climbed the stairs to the second floor.

They heard him say, "MRS. ADAMS! Why are YOU here again?

"Hey, what's that chair doing inside the closet?

"I bet you were looking for something on a shelf.

"Mrs. Adams, you're not here to decorate.

"You're looking for something.

"I bet it's the stamp collection! That's right, isn't it?"

They heard Mrs. Adams say, "Yes, that's

right, and I'm going to find it. Now get out of this house!"

Sammy said, "I'll tell April what you're doing."

Mrs. Adams said, "Go ahead. I'll tell her you're lying.

"She wouldn't believe YOU. You're just a child."

Sammy said, "I thought you said the stamps had been sold. I think YOU'RE the one who's been lying."

Mrs. Adams said, "Oh, stop wasting my time. Just GO!"

Sammy said, "If you want me to GO, then TELL me what's really going on!"

Mrs. Adams said, "OH, ALL RIGHT! I found a note on the dresser before April got here.

"But it didn't say where the stamps are. It didn't make any sense. He must have gone nutty as a bedbug, that stupid old man.

"Now go away!"

Sammy grinned.

He said, "What will you do if I DON'T go away? Call the police? Well, I'll do it for you."

He yelled, "Chief Hemster! Did you hear all that? Come on up!"

In a second, the chief was up the stairs.

Mrs. Adams stood still, looking pale as a ghost.

The chief said, "Mrs. Adams, give me the key to this house.

"Now get out of here before I arrest you. And never come back."

Slowly, she handed him the key.

She was too scared to talk.

Sammy made his scariest spider face as she walked out.

He felt a lot better.

The chief marched Mrs. Adams down the stairs and out the door.

Then Kathy said, "Hey, I think we should try to find that note.

"Maybe you could make some sense out of it, April."

Bill looked down at the wastebasket right next to the dresser.

There were little paper scraps in it.

Everyone went downstairs and pieced the scraps together on the table.

Mr. Fine pulled some clear tape out of his briefcase. They taped together the pieces.

Then April read them the note. It was a letter from her Grandpa Mugsy.

Chapter 13:
A Letter from Mugsy

April's hands shook as she held the patched-up letter.

She read out loud to them:

My Little April,

We planned to be together
in just a few weeks. But
some times plans don't work out.
I'm writing this letter to
remind you ofwhere the stamps
are. They'll be yours in case
any thing happens to me.
Remember, stamp collecting
takes many Twists and Turns;
you have to watch your Step,
every Second.
Love,
Mugsy

April said, "It's a letter from Papa Mugsy, all right.

"But I'm not sure what he meant to tell me.

"Poor Mugsy. He must have known he

was very sick."

Sammy said, "That letter doesn't sound like him.

"First, he says he's reminding you where the stamps are.

"Then he doesn't tell you where, after all!

"He was too sharp to do that by accident."

Dave looked at the letter for a minute and said, "I wonder why he put in those extra capitals.

"See, 'Twists and Turns' and 'Step and Second.'"

Sammy said, "Wait, I've heard those words before!

"He used to say them every time he went to get his stamps.

"'Stamp collecting takes many twists and turns. You have to watch your step, every second.'"

April said, "You know what? It seems to me I've heard those exact words, too ... years ago, when I was just a little girl.

"Why were they so important that he wrote them to me?"

Sammy said, "I don't know. All I know is he'd say that when he went up the stairs for his stamps."

April said, "The stairs! Up the stairs!"

Suddenly, she ran toward the second floor.

She stopped at the second step from the top and said, "SECOND STEP! TWIST AND TURN!"

She grabbed the post between the step and the railing.

She twisted it around. Then she turned it back.

They heard a soft click.

She grabbed hold of the step.

She lifted it like the lid of a toy chest.

The step was hollow!

The others crowded around to get a look inside.

The hollow ran back under the next step, too.

In it lay three big books, several boxes, and a pile of envelopes.

Sammy yelled, "You found it! It's Mugsy's collection!"

He turned and ran down the steps to tell Dave.

The others came down, too. They carried the whole stamp collection with them.

April said, "I don't know how to thank you all. And I don't know what to do with these stamps.

"I'd love to keep them here forever ... in the second-step hiding place.

"But I should protect them better than that.

"What do you think I should do, Mr. Fine?"

He said, "The first thing you should do is start calling me Sol, not Mr. Fine.

"Look through these stamps now, and

then put them back until morning.

"Tomorrow, place them in a safety-deposit box at the bank.

"Talk with an expert to decide which ones to sell.

"Then you can bring the rest back here."

April nodded. "OK, Sol. That sounds like a bright idea."

Dave said, "It ought to be bright. It's coming straight from the sun. That's what 'sol' means. It's another word for sun."

Sammy said, "Then I guess Mr. Fine WILL be hanging around.

"After all, a sun and a Moon sort of go together."

Mr. Fine said, "Sammy, you are a very smart young man."

April blushed and said, "Sammy if you weren't so wonderful, I'd say you're terrible!

"Now come help bring in the cookies I baked.

"We never had a chance to eat them at lunch."

Sammy hurried into the kitchen. "Hey, OATMEAL cookies!

"You're going to be one of the best neighbors I ever had!"

By the time he carried the platter in from the kitchen, he already had one cookie in his stomach ... and another one sticking out of his mouth.

He sat down, and everyone took a cookie.

Then the Woodland family and their friends sat talking and laughing and munching cookies all afternoon.